Annie Rose
Is My Little Sister

HARRISON COU
PUBLIC LIBRARY
105 North Capitol Ave
Corydon, IN 47112

Copyright © 2002 by Shirley Hughes
First published 2002 by Random House Children's Books U.K.

All rights reserved. No part of this book may be reproduced, transmitted, or stored in an information retrieval system
in any form or by any means, graphic, electronic, or mechanical, including photocopying, taping, and recording,
without prior written permission from the publisher.

First U.S. edition 2003

Library of Congress Cataloging-in-Publication Data

Hughes, Shirley, date.
Annie Rose is my little sister / Shirley Hughes. —1st U.S. ed.
p.   cm.
Summary: A boy describes all the things that he and his younger sister do together.
ISBN 0-7636-1959-0
[1. Brothers and sisters—Fiction.] I. Title.
PZ7.H87395 Amt 2003
[E]—dc21   2002067695

2 4 6 8 10 9 7 5 3 1

Printed and bound in Singapore by Tien Wah Press (Pte) Limited

This book was typeset in Bembo.
The artwork for this book was painted in gouache color
and oil pastels and finished with fine brushes.

Candlewick Press
2067 Massachusetts Avenue
Cambridge, Massachusetts 02140

visit us at www.candlewick.com

J FIC1-3

For Jack

Annie Rose
Is My Little Sister

Shirley Hughes

CANDLEWICK PRESS
CAMBRIDGE, MASSACHUSETTS

Annie Rose is my little sister.
She likes books a lot,
and she always wants me
to look at them with her.

She's good at playing games.
She likes it when I hide under a sheet
and peek out at her—Boo!

But when I'm really hiding,
she can hardly ever find me.

One of Annie Rose's favorite toys is her little chest of drawers. She likes opening and shutting each one.

She puts all sorts of things inside them.
Sometimes she pulls out all the drawers
and makes them into beds for her
family of mice.

The only things I have in my bed when I go
to sleep are my bit of blanket and my elephant,
Flumbo. He is quite old, nearly as old as I am.
But Annie Rose has lots of things
in her crib.

Early in the morning, I can hear her throwing them
out onto the floor, one by one—*thump, thump,
thump!* Then the only thing she has left in there is
Buttercup, her lamb. She doesn't often throw her out.

Annie Rose always wants to play with my toys.
She seems to like them better than her own—
and that is very annoying.

When I want to lay out all my cars and trucks
and train track, I have to put them on the table,
where Annie Rose can't get them.

Our favorite game to play together is store. When we have a store inside, we set out all the little packages and boxes and plastic bottles that Mom has saved for us, and we arrange all sorts of nice things on plates from Annie Rose's tea set.

Then I am the storekeeper, Mr. Lewis Burrows, and Annie Rose is my helper.

Sometimes Annie Rose wants to make her own
store in the backyard. She has leaf plates and sells
empty snail shells and daisies.

But she can't make a daisy chain. Neither can I.
Only Mom can do that.

When we go to the beach, Dad and I make a huge sandcastle with turrets and tunnels and a moat all around that fills up with water when the tide comes in. Annie Rose can only make sand pies. But they are very good ones.

Annie Rose doesn't like the ocean very much.
She prefers kicking up the water in shallow pools.

But Dad and I like diving into big, rough waves.

Annie Rose can be really awful sometimes.
She gets into a rage and lies on the floor and
screams and kicks. Most awful of all is when she
does this in a big store.

But after a while, she usually cheers up.

HARRISON COUNTY
PUBLIC LIBRARY
105 North Capitol Ave.
Corydon, IN 47112

Annie Rose's best friends are Marian and Lily.
They play together a lot. Sometimes—not very
often—Marian and Lily only want to play with
each other and they don't want Annie Rose.
That makes her very sad.

My best friend is Bernard. When he comes to play at our house, Annie Rose always wants to join in. She laughs and laughs when Bernard pretends to be a monster, showing its fierce teeth and making terrible noises.

Annie Rose loves Bernard.

But when Annie Rose cries,
or wakes up from her nap
in a bad mood, I'm
the only person who
can cheer her up.

Because she's my little sister,
and I'm her big brother,

and we'll go on being that forever . . .

. . . even until we're grown up.

DATE DUE			

J FIC 1-3 HUG

Hughes, Shirley, 1927-

Annie Rose is my little
 sister

NO CARD 2-23

HARRISON COUNTY
PUBLIC LIBRARY

Annie Rose is my little sister /
J FIC 1-3 HUG   54409

Hughes, Shirley,
HARRISON COUNTY PUBLIC LIBRARY